Let's go to the Circus

by LISL WEIL

HOLIDAY HOUSE / NEW YORK

for John

Copyright © 1988 by Lisl Weil
All rights reserved
Printed in the United States of America
First Edition

Library of Congress Cataloging-in-Publication Data

Weil, Lisl.
Let's go to the circus.

SUMMARY: Text and pictures present a history of
the circus from its origins in ancient Rome.
1. Circus—History—Juvenile literature.
[1. Circus—History] I. Title.
GV1817.W45 1988   791.3   87-25201
ISBN 0-8234-0693-8

Let's go to the

Circus

Everyone loves to go to the circus.
It is a wonderland for all ages.
Who doesn't want to be a ringmaster,
at least once?

The circus is filled with glitter and excitement.
There's plenty to see and plenty of snacks to eat—
           pretzels, popcorn, peanuts,
           hot dogs, ice cream, and cotton candy.
           There are sodas and drinks, too.
           And there are lots and lots of people.

But the circus wasn't always
so filled with joy.

More than 2,000 years ago, Roman families went to the circus to see men fighting animals in contests of strength. The crowds also watched chariot races and performances by athletes and gymnasts. They sat in galleries around a ring in an enormous building that could hold as many as 50,000 people.

The ring—or circle—is what gave the circus its name.

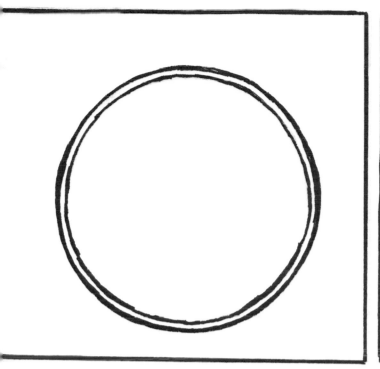

Horses and Performers had their quarters below.

THE ANCIENT ROMAN CIRCUS

By the middle of the first century, fighting games became very cruel. Under Emperor Nero, the Circus Maximus, which seated 250,000 people, was one of the cruelest. But when the Roman Empire came to an end in A.D. 476, the cruelty stopped and so did the circus. Then, for centuries, there was no circus. Instead, during the Middle Ages, people in Europe were entertained by minstrels—travelling musicians who played instruments like the lute or recorder. Kings, queens, and nobles liked to listen to troubadours— poets who recited long love poems, often set to music.

MINSTRELS

TROUBADOUR

From ancient times onward, there was one performer who always made people laugh. At first, he was called simply a fool.

But later, in the 1700s, he was called a buffoon or a jester. He was admired for his wit and his wisdom all through the Middle Ages, and was honored in the courts of Europe by the royal families he served. With his colorful costume and jingly bells, the fool was the ancestor of the clown.

At the end of the eighteenth century, the circus came to life again. An Englishman, Philip Astley, performed tricks on the backs of two or three horses that he rode at full gallop. His show became so successful that he later added tightrope walkers and dancing dogs. This is why he is now thought of as "the father of the circus."

an equestrian act at
Franconi's Circus in Paris.

Over the next fifty years, big cities in America, England,
Europe, and Russia created their own circuses. They took
place in amphitheaters—buildings large enough to have such
grand shows with their many acts. Performers joined the
circuses from all over the world.

But many farmers and other Americans lived too far from the cities to get to the circus. Tent shows were started that could travel to small towns all over the country. Eager crowds lined the roads and streets, waiting for the decorated wagons to parade by.

They watched as the circus men put up the tents and filled the horse ring with sawdust. They listened to the strange animal noises and tapped their feet to the loud circus music coming from the steam calliope or *orchestmelochor* wagon.

There were many fine small and large travelling tent shows, but the first famous American circus owner was James A. Bailey. He began his life as an orphan and worked his way up to owning Cooper & Bailey, one of the biggest circuses in the world at that time.

The most imaginative American circus was run by Phineas T. Barnum. He thought up wonderful acts. He was famous for introducing the world to Tom Thumb, the tiniest person to ever perform. Mr. Barnum and Mr. Bailey joined forces in 1881, and "The Greatest Show on Earth" was born.

The Barnum & Bailey circus had three rings and travelled around the country in three tents. It also had marvelous sideshows outside the "Big Top," as the main tent of the circus came to be called. People flocked to see the fat lady, the strong man, and other attractions. In 1907 Barnum & Bailey's show was bought by the Ringling Brothers, who had their own very famous and successful circus.

THE RINGLING BROTHERS-Barnum & Bailey Circus

is still one of the grandest in the world. No longer performed in tents, it plays in large buildings in big cities, just as the circus did in the nineteenth century. Attractions of daring

and beauty that were popular then still dazzle crowds today. Although costumes may be more elaborate now, the circus parade that enters the city before the opening of the show continues to be free. And the lady shot from a cannon or the elegant acts on horseback continue to hold audiences spellbound.

What would a circus be without the elephants marching around the ring in time to the brass band's music?

Holding on to each other's tails with their trunks, they also balance light-footed performers on their backs.

The audience loves to watch the clowns. They make everyone laugh and have a good time. There are fat, thin, small, big, happy, sad, male, and female clowns. Sometimes, one of the clown's children or a small animal joins the act. Each clown paints on his own face and designs his own costume. No other clown may use the same face.

The trainers and their trained animals are a spectacle that fills everyone with awe. Who doesn't gasp when he sees the lion tamer stare into the jaws of a lion! It is the trainer's love, trust, and patience—not his whip—that make the animals perform so well.

When the daring trapeze artists fly way up high over the ring, catching one another just in time, people cover their eyes in fright!

The acrobats' act is one of everyone's favorites. Their balance and skill take long hours of practice. The performers depend on each other, just as close families do. No wonder that there are "circus families" with performers in generation after generation.

The circus has other remarkable acts of skill, too—and always, the audience is thrilled and excited.

The workers behind the lights are just as important as the stars out front. They are in charge of setting up the acts. They have to make sure that everything goes safely and smoothly. Like the performers, the workers often belong to families that have been with the circus generation after generation.

The circus, then, is really a family affair—families performing and families watching. Old and young alike laugh together as they enjoy what truly remains "The Greatest Show on Earth."

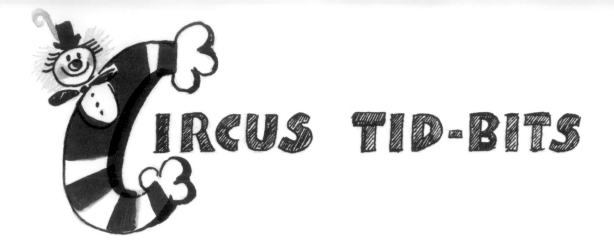

CIRCUS TID-BITS

The first American circus was produced by John Bill Ricketts in Philadelphia in 1793. President Washington went to it.

The first modern circus performances in New York were at the Hippodrome in 1893 and at Niblo's Garden. In Philadelphia, the first modern circus was at the Chestnut Theater in 1830. In Los Angeles, the Norris & Howe Circus performed in 1909.

Admission was only 50 cents!

In the early 1900s, there were different kinds of travelling circuses. The Spalding & Rogers Floating Circus Palace travelled along waterways instead of roads.

The Wild West circus shows were very popular. One of the stars was Annie Oakley. A child of the frontier, she was a sharp-shooter. It was said she could hit a fifty-cent piece from thirty feet away. The musical play *Annie Get Your Gun* tells her story.

Annie Oakley

BUFFALO BILL

Another idol of the Wild West shows was Buffalo Bill. His curled hair, good looks, and beautiful costumes were admired by all, and he was a hero to young boys.

The largest circus animal ever shown was Jumbo, a six-and-a-half ton African elephant. King Tusk, with the Ringling Bros. and Barnum & Bailey Circus, is considered the biggest performing elephant alive today.

The first famous elephant shown in America was "Old Bet." The Elephant Hotel, now a community center in Somers, New York, was built and named for her.

Gunther Gebel-Williams is one of the circus's most famous animal trainers. Employed by The Ringling Bros. and Barnum & Bailey, he trains tigers, elephants, and horses. His wife Sigrid has trained her own group of performing horses and his daughter Tina has a ringful of Russian wolfhounds.

Emmett Kelly (1898–1979), a famous clown, created a character named "Weary Willie."